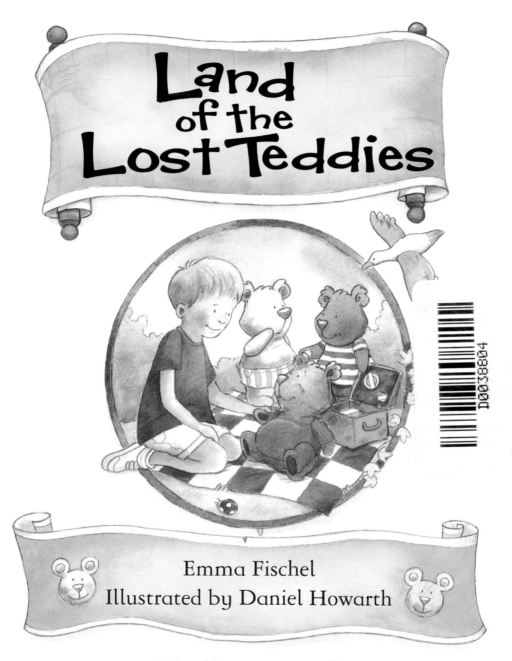

Land
of the
Lost Teddies

Emma Fischel

Illustrated by Daniel Howarth

Edited by Louie Stowell
Cover design by Will Dawes

Contents

Off to Fun World

Wilfie and his teddy, Eddie, are excited about their trip to Fun World. But little do they know quite how exciting their day will be...

Where's Eddie?

At Fun World, Wilfie and
Eddie bounced...

and
whooshed...

and won a prize.

They even went
looking for sharks
in the bay.

But suddenly, Wilfie cried, "Where's
Eddie?" All he could see were his
teddy's sunglasses and
one of his shoes.

Can you spot them?

The search begins

Wilfie tried to cheer himself up with a trip to the toy shop, but looking at other teddies just made him sadder about Eddie.

"You could try looking in the Land of the Lost Teddies," said the toy shop owner. "Most teddies go there when children lose them." He opened the green door behind him. "And there's a train going there now."

The toy shop owner scratched his head. "But I can't remember which train it is. It has a shape on the front, but not a star, and a blue funnel. And the engine is red."

Which train should Wilfie take?

On the train

The conductor blew her whistle and they were off. The train chugged past Spook Castle and Jelly Town.

As they puffed past Shipville, Wilfie asked the conductor where he should get off.
"Just after Teddy Tunnel," she replied.

How many more stops are there before the tunnel?

Which way now?

When Wilfie reached the Land of the Lost Teddies, he gasped. "How am I going to find Eddie here? There are teddies EVERYWHERE!"

Wilfie didn't know where to begin to look for Eddie. Then he spotted something that gave him a clue.

What has Wilfie seen? It's one of a pair, and Wilfie has the other one!

Picnic path

Wilfie followed the path where he'd found the shoe until he reached a big iron gate. He read the notice and beamed. "Eddie loves picnics. I bet I'll find him there!"

Can you help Wilfie get to the picnic?

PICNIC TODAY
IN MIDDLE
OF MAZE
start at the
red flag

START

Teddy Bears' Picnic

At the picnic, Wilfie could see big teddies, small teddies, old teddies... but not HIS teddy. He took out his photo of Eddie. Perhaps someone had seen him.

"Yes, we've seen him," said a yellow teddy. "That's the bear who ate all the pizza. AND the last slice of chocolate cake."

FIND THE ODD ONE OUT

"We'll tell you where he went if you solve this puzzle for us," said a purple teddy bear.

Which clown is the odd one out?

Bear trouble

"He's at the lake just up the road... but don't get lost," said the yellow bear. "Or you might end up on Bear Mountain. The bears there are big. VERY big."

Wilfie walked on. Was this the right path? It seemed very steep.

It grew colder and colder. Soon it began to snow.

The path grew steeper and steeper.

OOPS! Wilfie bumped into something. A very large, furry something. Something like a **VERY BIG BEAR.** "What's it going to do?" Wilfie thought.

GROWL?

ROAR?

OR EAT ME?

The bear cave

"Don't be afraid, I just need help," said the bear. It held out its paw. It had a thorn stuck in it. Wilfie pulled it out as gently as he could. The bear asked him to tea to say thank you.

"Just hop on my back!" What a ride! Wilfie clung on tightly to the bear's warm fur.

They stopped at the bear's cave and went in for tea. Wilfi told the bear about h lost teddy.

"Eddie?" said the bear. "I took him to the lake because he wanted to take a boat to Mermaid Island. Oh, and he dropped something..."

Can you see what Eddie left behind?

By the lake

After a big plate of honey buns the bear took Wilfie to the lake. "Good luck finding Eddie," said the bear.

BOAT TRIPS

TODAY

BOATS TO ~ATE ~AND

BOATS TO MERMAID ISLAND

BOATS TO DINOSAUR ISLAND

FULL

FULL

FULL

FULL

FULL

FULL

FULL

"Which boat should I take to Mermaid Island?" Wilfie asked the boat keeper.

"There's only one boat left that goes there," the man replied. He pointed at the pictures on his board. "The others are full."

Which boat can Wilfie take to Mermaid Island?

Mermaid Island

When Wilfie reached
Mermaid Island he
searched for Eddie...

high...

and low.

"Found him!"
thought Wilfie.

But he was wrong.
It was a merteddy!

Wilfie showed him Eddie's photo. "I've seen that bear," replied the merteddy. "He went across the rocks. A snapping crab took a piece out of his shorts!"

Can you find a safe way to the shore avoiding rocks with crabs on them?

Another clue

Wilfie trudged on. There was no sign of Eddie. But he saw a little pair of yellow shorts sticking out of a garbage can. They were Eddie's.

SLEEPY SAM'S
PJ STALL

SWEETS

BURGERS

HOSPITAL

NURSERY

PLAYGROUND

ICES

ICES

ICES

The teddy at the clothes stall said that
Eddie had bought a sleepsuit from him so
he could go to the nursery for a nap.
"What a fussy teddy he was! He wanted
stripes, but not yellow ones... something
blue, but not with red, and nothing green!"

Which outfit do you think Eddie chose?

Bedtime Story

Wilfie ran to the nursery and knocked. There was no answer, so he pushed open the door. Would he find Eddie at last?

   Inside, Wilfie saw sleepy teds tucked up in bed and storytime teds listening to a tale. But, best of all, Wilfie could see HIS ted!

Where's Eddie? Who's the storyteller?

Teddy's story

Wilfie hugged his teddy tightly.
"However did you get here, Eddie?"
Eddie began to tell his story...

A huge seagull snatched me up.

He dropped me as soon as he realized I wasn't a nice juicy fish.

I landed on a porpoise. He took me to the shore.

I found a train station, but no one was around.

There was a box of blankets. I nodded off in it.

I woke up on a train. It was going to the Land of the Lost Teddies.

Then, they decided it was time to go home. The toy shop keeper had gifts for them... if only he could remember where he'd put them.

Can you spot the presents?

Homeward bound

On the train home, they opened their presents. But Wilfie thought that the best present was having Eddie back with him again.